O9-AHT-070

VALENTINE'S DAY FROM THE BLACK LAGOON®

VALENTINE'S DAY FROM THE BLACK LAGOON®

by Mike Thaler

Illustrated by Jared Lee

SCHOLASTIC INC.

New York Toronto London Auckland Sydney
Mexico City New Delhi Hong Kong Buenos Aires

To Elisabeth and Hope, Heart to heart—M.T.
To Vicki Ketterman, My art school valentine—J.L.

visit us at www.abdopublishing.com

Reinforced library bound edition published in 2014 by Spotlight, a division of the ABDO Group, PO Box 398166, Minneapolis, MN 55439. Spotlight produces high-quality reinforced library bound editions for schools and libraries. Published by agreement with Scholastic, Inc.

Printed in the United States of America, North Mankato, Minnesota.
102013
012014

This book contains at least 10% recycled materials.

Cataloging-in-Publication Data

Thaler, Mike, 1936-
Valentine's Day from the Black Lagoon / by Mike Thaler ; illustrated by Jared Lee.
p. cm. -- (Black Lagoon adventures; #8)
Summary: Hubie learns about love while trying to decide to whom he should give a valentine.
1. Valentine's Day--Juvenile fiction. 2. School--Juvenile fiction. 3. Monsters--Juvenile fiction. I. Title. II Series.
PZ7.T3 Va 2006
[Fic]--dc23

ISBN 978-1-61479-209-3 (Reinforced Library Bound Edition)

All Spotlight books are reinforced library binding and manufactured in the United States of America.

CONTENTS

CHAPTER 1
LOVE, YUCK!

Valentine's Day is a week away. Mrs. Green says we're going to have a party. And if that's not bad enough, we have to exchange valentine cards—with girls! Yuck!

I'm too young for this. I know how it goes. First you give a girl a valentine card, then she wants to hold your hand, and before you know it—you're married.

LUNCH MENU
OH, NO.

And what if I give one to a girl who doesn't give me one back? Oh, the pain! Oh, the hurt! Oh, the embarrassment! Oh, the rejection!

Maybe I can be out sick on Friday . . . HEARTSICK!

CHAPTER 2
HEARTICHOKES

On the school bus, Penny and Doris sit down on either side of me. They start telling me about their dolls—I'm moving! I go to the back of the bus, but they follow me.

T. Rex, our bus driver, tells us to stop changing seats, so I'm stuck with them for eight blocks. *What* do they *want*?

"Who are you going to give a valentine to Hubie?" asks Doris, fluttering her eyelashes at me. The heart is out of the bag.

"I don't know," I answer.

"My name has two *n*'s," says Penny. Now *she* flutters her eyelashes at me.

"I know," I reply.

"My name doesn't have any *n*'s," blurts Doris.

"That's nice," I answer.

Luckily we arrive at my stop and I bolt for the door. I'm out and still single. They're both waving and winking at me from the back window as the bus pulls away. The pressure has already started.

CHAPTER 3
MATTERS OF THE HEART

As soon as I get home, I explain the situation to my mom. She says that I should be flattered that they fluttered.

"But, Mom, I can't give both of them a card," I say. "It would be *big-of-me*."

"When I was a little girl, I had a crush on Henry Stillman," replies Mom. "I followed him around everywhere. Then, on Valentine's Day, he gave a card to Nancy Dringle. It broke my heart —until I got a card from Freddy Farkle. I didn't even know he liked me."

"What happened?" I ask.

"He was hurt because I didn't give him a card."

"It sounds like a mess," I say.

"It's called *love*, Hubie."

CHAPTER 4
WHAT IS THIS THING CALLED LOVE?

That evening I watch some TV and try to find out what love is. I watch *The Love Boat*, *Love Story*, and *The Valentine's Day Massacre*.

Boy, love *is* messy. I'd like to go to Tibet and sit in a cave until Valentine's Day is over. I'll come back for Christmas.

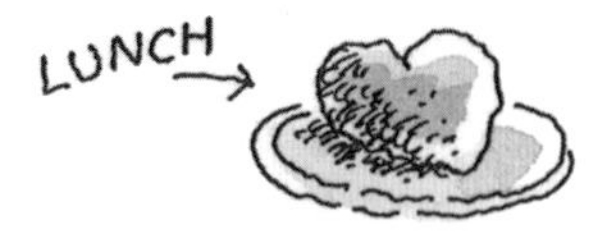

CHAPTER 5
EAT YOUR HEART OUT

Later that night, I have a HEARTMARE! A mad scientist named Dr. Love injects a chicken heart with some growth hormones.

It's in a jar, beating loudly. But soon it fills up the jar, lifts the lid, and bubbles out all over the counter.

Now Dr. Love has his heart on his sleeve. And soon he's absorbed in his work. But the heart keeps growing with every beat, and now it fills the room. It breaks through the wall and thumps out onto the highway. It squashes a lot of cars, which turns into a major traffic jam.

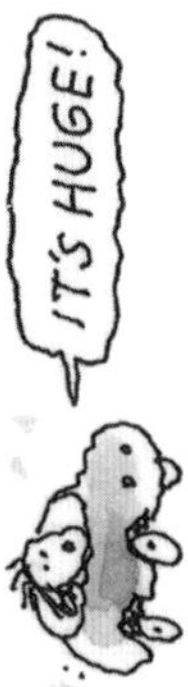

I'm home in bed and I hear a loud thumping. I peer out the window and see this giant heart coming down my street, murmuring . . .

"Hubie . . . Hubie . . . Hubie, wake up! It's time for school."

Phew, it's only Mom.

CHAPTER 6
STONE HEART

On the school bus, I don't sit near any girls. All of us guys huddle in the back of the bus.

"So," says Eric, "who are you going to give your valentine card to?"

"I'm giving mine to Penny," says Derrick.

"I'm giving mine to Doris," says Randy.

"I'm baking cookies for everybody," says Freddy.

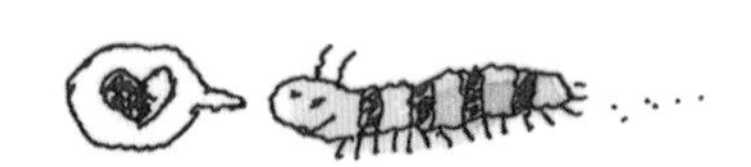

"What about you, Hubie?" everyone asks.

Suddenly, the bus is quiet. All heads turn toward me. My heart is in my mouth.

"I don't know," I mumble.

"That's a half-hearted answer," replies Eric.

"Take heart," comments Derrick.

"Let's get to the heart of the matter," says Randy.

I think I'm having a heart attack.

CHAPTER 7
CUPID IS STUPID

In art class, we all have to make hearts. Each one has to be the same shape, and either red or pink. Yuck! I say that I want to make a green-colored square one.

Mrs. Swamp, our art teacher, says, "No, only a heart shape, and either pink or red."

The shape doesn't leave a lot of room for creativity. Well, at least I'll draw a dinosaur on mine.

"No," says Mrs. Swamp. "A dinosaur is not appropriate. You can either draw a cupid or flowers."

Double yuck—I'd rather eat worms.

Mrs. Swamp says that we can't even draw any veins or blood. This is not freedom of expression. I feel wounded. I think I need a purple heart.

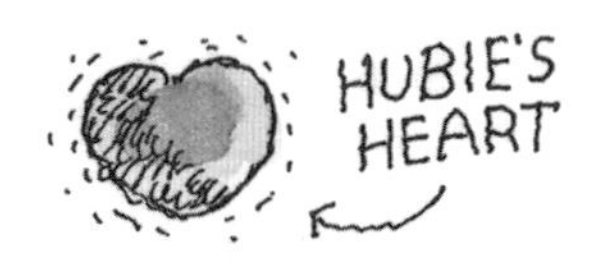

CHAPTER 8
A CHANGE OF HEART

Back inside our classroom, everything suddenly changes. Mr. Bender, our principal, brings in a new student. Her name is Tiffany Hart. She has blond curls, blue eyes, and pink lips. She is beautiful! I think I am really having a heart attack!

I look around. All the guys are looking at her, too. Their eyes are bulging and their mouths are wide open. Hey, I saw her first. I feel jealous already.

"There's an empty seat next to me!" I blurt out.

Mrs. Green brings her over and gives her the desk next to mine. Tiffany smells like flowers. I sniff the air.

"My name is Tiffany," she says with a smile.

"My name's Tiffany, too," I say. "I mean, Hubie."

"Nice to meet you, Hubie," she says, holding out her hand. I can't shake it. My hand is sweating. I wipe it on my shirt, and we shake hands. Wow! It's like putting your fingers into an electric socket!

I can't let go. She smiles again and flutters her long eyelashes.

I'm falling . . . I'm falling . . . I'm falling in love.

CHAPTER 9
HEART DREAMS

I'm ready to slay dragons for her, climb mountains, and swim the seven seas. I'd even marry her if she asked me. Of course, I'd have to ask my mom first. We *can't elope* because then we'd be melons.

At lunch, she sits with the girls—traitors. I try to hear what they're saying. All I hear is giggling. Uh-oh, I just ate my napkin. Well, I wasn't hungry anyway. My stomach is on a trampoline, and my heart is on my sleeve.

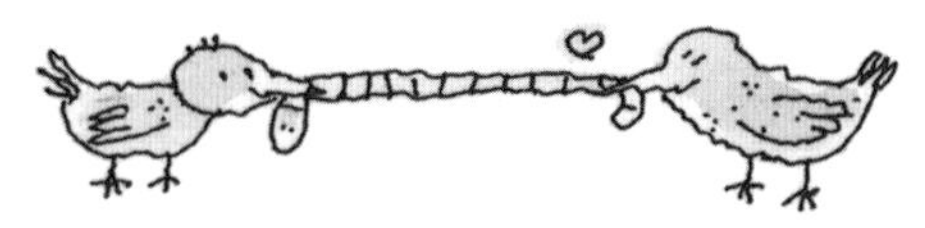

I look around. None of the guys are eating either, except for Freddy. Nothing stands between him and food. And now he's eating everyone else's lunch, too. But no one cares.

Hey, they're all in love with *my* girl. But how can I win her heart? There are no dragons to slay, no mountains to climb, and no seas to swim. I know! I'll make her an incredible Valentine's Day card.

But first I have to go to the library and do a little research.

CHAPTER 10
RESEARCHING THE HEART

After lunch, I go visit Mrs. Beamster, our librarian, and tell her my problem. She gives me a book called *Romance Through the Ages*.

It starts with Stone Age courtship. If a caveman loved a cavelady, he'd grab her by the hair and drag her off to his cave. I could try that at recess, but I think I'd get sent to the principal's office. And what if she is wearing a wig?

In the Middle Ages, knights would save their ladies from dragons. I knew that.

In the Romantic Age, guys would put their jackets over muddy puddles so that girls wouldn't get their feet wet. If I brought home a muddy jacket, my mom would kill me.

ROMEO WAS LATE FOR DINNER AND JULIET IT ALL.

Men also wrote lots of poems. It was the age of *puddles* and *poems*. Then later, troubadours would play guitars and sing under a lady's balcony.

I wonder if Tiffany has a balcony. I don't play the guitar, but I am taking piano lessons.

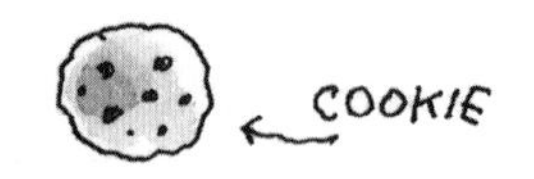

In modern courtship, men send flowers, candy, and diamond rings. With my allowance, I could give her a chocolate-chip cookie. Boy, courtship sounds like a real trial.

CHAPTER 11
HAPPILY NEVER AFTER

In class, Mrs. Green tells us stories about famous romances. There was Romeo and Juliet. They fell in love, but their families didn't get along. Juliet had a balcony, but it still didn't work out.

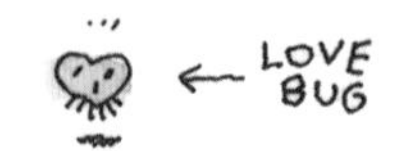

Then there was Anthony and Cleopatra. She was bitten by the love bug, but unfortunately, she was also bitten by a snake.

Love is an enormous mess. I hope it goes better for Tiffany and Hubie.

CHAPTER 12
POURING OUT YOUR HEART

After school, I empty out my piggy bank and go to the art store. I've turned into a *romaniac*. I buy the biggest piece of pink paper I can find. This is going to be larger than the monstrous chicken heart from my nightmare.

HUBIE HAS A HEART OF..... ① GOLD ② SILVER ③ IRON ④ PLASTIC
(ANSWER ON PAGE 52)

I buy lace, silver glitter, and glue. And I have enough money left over for a blue pen. I tell the salesman it's all for my mother.

I carefully carry everything home, get a pair of scissors, and lock myself in my room. I cut out a giant heart. What a wonderful shape! What a beautiful color!

I take my new blue pen and draw Cupid. As I remember, a cupid is a little baby with wings, wearing a diaper and holding a bow. He shoots arrows into your heart and you're in love.

That's the way I feel about Tiffany. What a beautiful name—I just love to say it.

"Tiffany, Tiffany, Tiffany . . . !" I exclaim. Cupid has hurled a harpoon into *my* heart.

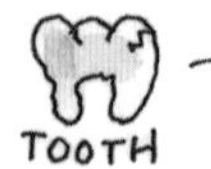

→ A HEARTACHE IS LIKE A TOOTHACHE ONLY IT HURTS INSIDE.

CHAPTER 13
CUT TO THE QUICK

On the school bus in the morning, Tiffany is sitting between Eric and Derrick. She's smiling at both of them and doesn't even notice when I get on. I sit down two rows behind them.

Eric is telling her jokes. She's laughing. How could they do this to me? I hate Eric. His jokes aren't even funny. Besides, I've heard them all before.

MICKEY MANTLE

Derrick is showing off. He's pulling out all his baseball cards. I'll really hate him if he shows her his 1952 Mickey Mantle rookie card. Then I'm sunk.

Tiffany doesn't even turn around to look at me. Now I hate her.

When the school bus stops, I walk right by her. I'll show her!

I won't even say, "Hello!" if she says, "Hello!"

She doesn't even bother. That's it—we're through!

The dragons can have her. She can climb up her own mountains. She can swim across her own seas. I want a divorce!

CHAPTER 14
HEARTBURN

At lunch, Tiffany sits down next to me. I get up and move my tray to another table. That'll teach her a lesson. Now she's sitting at the table alone. Good! That'll teach her to break my heart.

ANSWER: GOLD

← RAIN DROP ← TEAR

There's a tear running down her cheek. I'm about to go back when Eric and Derrick sit down next to her. In no time, she's laughing.

It's probably at the same jokes she heard this morning. She wipes her cheek and puts her nose in the air.

Falling in love is easy . . . it's landing that's hard!

I've lost Tiffany for good. And now, I'm stuck with a four-foot-tall valentine card!

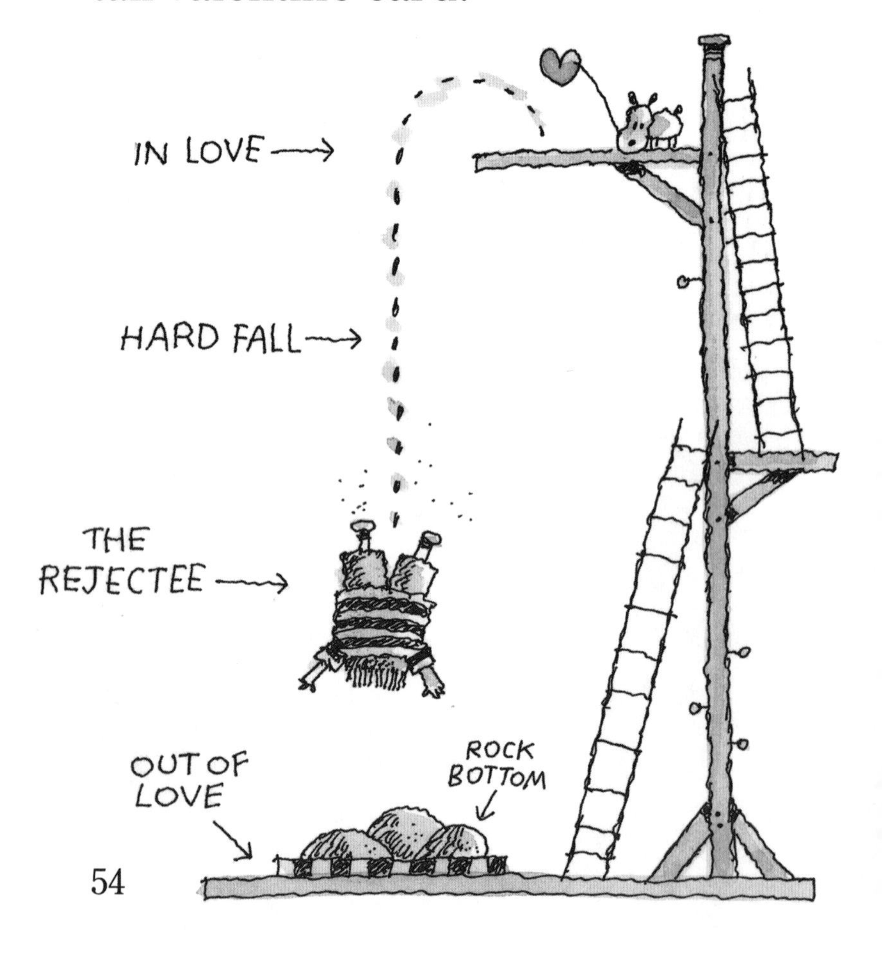

CHAPTER 15
HEARTFELT

I don't talk to anyone for the rest of the day. When a heart breaks, it leaves sharp pieces. I head straight home after school. It's good to get back home, into my own room, and onto my own bed.

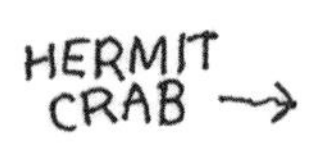

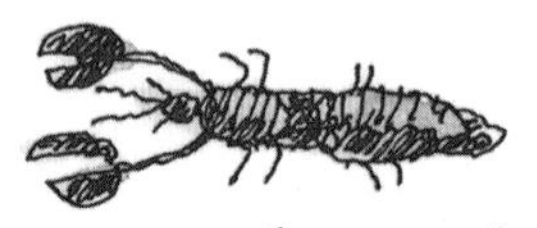

I think I'll become a hermit. I'll go live in a cave, one without bats. My friends will all be sorry. One day they will miss me. I start to daydream . . .

ANSWER: A HAMPHIBIAN

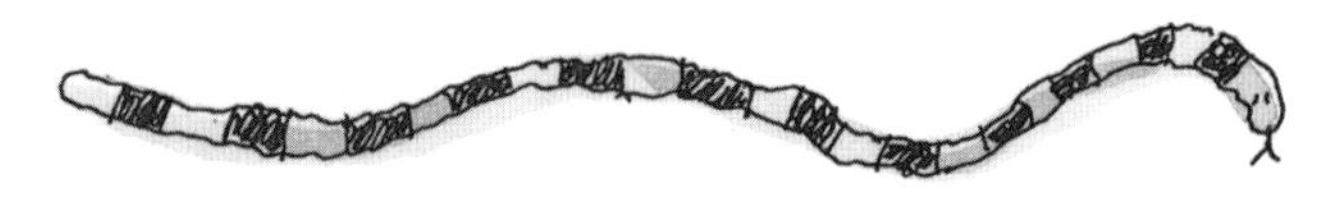

Eric will ask, "What ever happened to Hubie?"

"He missed the Valentine's Day party," Derrick will answer.

"I still have his cookie," Freddy will announce.

"Let's go find him," they will all agree.

So they'll set out to find me. They'll swim a sea. They'll climb a mountain and they'll find me sitting on a stalagmite. Or is it a stalactite? I can never remember which one hangs from the ceiling, and which one grows up from the ground.

“We miss you,” they will say.

“Won’t you come back?” they will plead.

“We have a heart-shaped cookie for you,” Freddy will say. “It got a little wet when we swam the sea, but it is still good.”

"What ever happened to Tiffany?" I will ask.

"Oh, she married Henry Stillman," they will answer.

"My mom was in love with Henry Stillman," I will say. "Love is very confusing."

SOGGY COOKIE

"No, it's simple. You are our friend, and we love you," they will all shout with huge smiles.

Freddy will hand me a soggy cookie. . . .

Hey, tomorrow's Valentine's Day. I get a pair of scissors. I've still got a lot of work to do.

CHAPTER 16
WITH ALL ONE'S HEART

Mrs. Green has decorated our room with lots of hearts. Freddy's cookies are on a paper heart-shaped party platter.

We sing the old Beatles' song "All You Need Is Love." Now it is time to exchange cards.

I have one for everyone in our class. I hand them all out. I'm glad that I bought such a big piece of paper. Many hearts came from one.

I even give a card to Mrs. Green. It makes her smile. I wrote on it . . .

Roses are red
Violets are blue
I want to be a teacher
Just like you!

I did get some cards, too. Including one from Tiffany!

But you know what I learned?

It's really more important what you give, than what you get. Also, I learned that a big heart goes a long way.